Scene

Leonardo DiCaprio

Kieran Scott

Aladdin Paperbacks

FOR BOO

First Aladdin Paperbacks edition September 1998

Cover photo: ©1997 by Armando Gallo/Retna Limited, USA.

Text copyright ©1998 by Daniel Weiss Associates, Inc.

Produced by 17th Street Productions, a division of Daniel Weiss Associates, Inc. 33 West 17th Street New York, NY 10011

Aladdin Paperbacks An imprint of Simon & Schuster Children's Publishing Division 1230 Avenue of the Americas New York, NY 10020

Designed by Michael Rivilis Printed and bound in the United States of America 10 9 8 7 6 5 4 3 2

Library of Congress Catalog Card Number 98-73015

ISBN 0-689-82404-1

Leo at the *Titanic* premiere.

Leo

Rising

Leonardo DiCaprio is the ultimate romantic hero, the most sought-after young movie star, one of the most gifted actors of his generation . . . and a complete goofball.

Tales of Leo's antics are legendary throughout Hollywood. On the set he keeps himself occupied by impersonating his fellow actors and crew members, playing practical jokes, and generally cutting up.

Leo has always been known for his joking ways. As a young boy he would entertain his classmates by doing Michael Jackson impressions in the school yard. But back then he never could have imagined that he would one day be improvising one-man shows in front of award-winning actors like Gabriel Byrne, Jeremy Irons, Gérard Depardieu, and John Malkovich as he did on the set of *The Man in the Iron Mask*. Talk about an intimidating audience.

But that didn't stop Leonardo DiCaprio. "Late one night we were shooting a death scene, and it required the highest level of emotional intensity," says Randall Wallace, the film's director. "Just as I'm about to yell 'Action,' I notice Leo has a celery stick sticking out of his iron mask."

Leo moon-walked between takes of the famous trellis scene in *William Shakespeare's Romeo and Juliet* and impersonated James Cameron, the director of *Titanic*. He was even a

Leo with Gwyneth Paltrow.

5

©1994 by Steve Granitz/Retna Ltd.

Leo at the 1994 Academy Awards.

"OUTSIDE THE HOUSE HE MAY BE FAMOUS, BUT INSIDE HE'S NO LONGER FAMOUS. HE'S JUST LEO THE JERK, LIKE US."

—pal Jonah Johnson

prankster on the set of *Growing Pains*, way back when he was sixteen.

Leonardo says he likes to run around the set to keep his energy going, and Kate Winslet and Danny Nucci, his costars from *Titanic*, claim that his attitude is infectious. Given the serious nature of the roles Leo has played, one has to wonder if he doesn't need to be silly between takes in order to keep sane. Half the time he's in front of the camera, he's crying (*What's Eating Gilbert Grape?*), overdosing (*The Basketball Diaries*), dying (*William Shakespeare's Romeo and Juliet*, *Titanic*), or

Leo tries to keep up with the latest fashions, and he does his best to support charities . . . which is probably why he attended the Race to Erase MS benefit in L.A. The event included a Tommy Hilfiger fashion show and performances by No Doubt and Sheryl Crow.

trying to save someone (*Titanic*, *The Man in the Iron Mask*). It must take a lot out of him. But don't expect Leo to give up serious roles anytime soon.

"I want to go with things that have integrity and that I feel I'm doing for me," Leonardo says. To Leo, this means taking roles that challenge him rather than focusing on films that will simply make a lot of money. So what, you might ask, was Leonardo doing in the record-breaking, box-office-smashing, biggest money grosser of all time— the unstoppable *Titanic*? Well, he didn't expect the insanity the film caused, but he took it all in stride.

At the Los Angeles premiere of *Titanic*, as fans screamed behind him, Leo said, "I'm

overwhelmed. I've never made a movie of this caliber. It's pretty spectacular. But I just try to keep it real."

Later he told *E!* that he didn't think he'd be doing another blockbuster-size film in the near future. "After the whole experience, I know it's really not my cup of tea—all respect to . . . the actors who do that type of thing." Ever the individual, Leonardo is much more comfortable in small independent films like those he's made in the past, which don't necessarily attract a large audience. And yet with Leo's current level of popularity, it's hard to imagine his films will ever have problems bringing in moviegoers again.

In its 1998 spring movie preview issue, *Entertainment Weekly* put it quite nicely: "After *Titanic*, DiCaprio could probably sell tickets to a documentary about belly button lint."

And knowing Leo, he'd find a way to make it a hit.

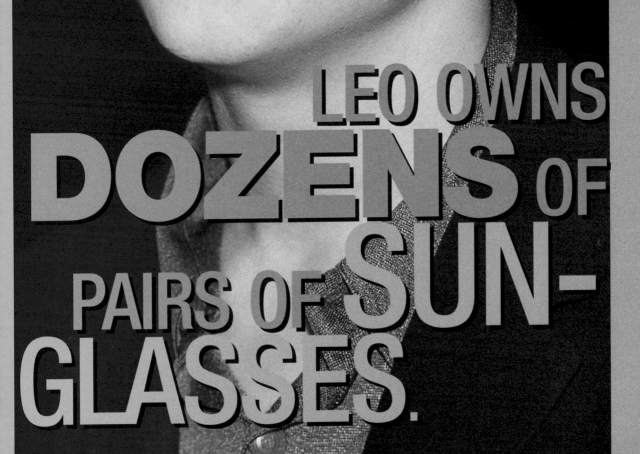

LEO OWNS **DOZENS** OF **PAIRS OF SUN-GLASSES.**

From Tiny Tot

©Darlene Hammond/Archive Photos

It's no wonder that Leonardo Wilhelm DiCaprio grew up to be such an honest and emotional actor. Born to hippie parents on November 11, 1974, in Los Angeles, California, Leo was brought up without much money but with a lot of love and support. His parents raised him to love animals, museums, and foreign cultures. His mother, Irmelin, was born and bred in Germany before moving to L.A. and settling down with Leo's father, George DiCaprio. As a young boy, Leonardo traveled to his mother's native land and loved it. This led to his dream of traveling all over the world.

to TV

"**W**hen I was young, I used to have this thing where I wanted to see everything. I used to think, 'How can I die without seeing every inch of this world?'" Leo says. As an actor he's been able to make this dream come true, traveling to Cannes film festivals, *Titanic* premieres in Tokyo and London, rehearsals for *Romeo and Juliet* in Australia, and location shoots in Mexico, Paris, and all over the United States.

But as a child, Leonardo was lucky just to get out of his neighborhood. His parents separated when he was still a baby, and he and his mother settled down in Hollywood. But it wasn't the glamorous city you might imagine it to be. Leonardo was surrounded by harsh images of real life—drug dealers and people living on the streets.

"I just had to stay tough and develop a plan for doing something better with my life than what kids were doing all around me," Leo says. To keep him safe from the rough influences in the 'hood, Leo's mom sent him to school in Westwood—a more upscale area of Los Angeles and a one-hour drive from his home each way.

Leo's father was a dedicated parent as well. Even though he didn't live with Leo and his mom and eventually remarried, George DiCaprio was always a huge part of Leonardo's life.

"I think what I liked best about my childhood was the repetitiveness of the things we did. I think when you're a kid, and you do a whole bunch of things, it's all a blur and you really don't remember anything. But we did the same things—went to the same museums, took the same pony

rides—and those things have become locked in my memory as one good experience," Leo told *Vanity Fair*. "My parents are so a part of my life that they're like my legs or something. . . . And it wasn't like they created a false good time—that they went out of their way to show me fabulous things. It was just that they were around and they were great."

Some of his fondest childhood memories come from his birthday parties at a train museum in California. During an interview with *Premiere* in 1996 Leo took the reporter, along with Claire Danes, to the museum and pointed out the picnic area between old abandoned engines where the

Leo in earlier years.

©Darlene Hammond/Archive Photos

een

9

parties used to take place. "Every year all my friends would climb up on that trolley car and hang off it while my mom took a picture," Leo told them.

Even though Leo loved museums and history, he wasn't

Leo at the *What's Eating Gilbert Grape?* premiere (above). Leo with Kirk Cameron during the days of *Growing Pains* (left).

exactly the model student. Just as he's active during filming now, he had a hard time sitting still in school. "A lot of times school is just so dull and boring, it's hard for a kid to learn in that environment," Leo says. "There's hardly any vibrance there." It seems all Leo needed was a more interactive education. As soon as he began acting and was taught by an on-set tutor, his grades skyrocketed.

While Leonardo grew to love learning, his real passion was performing—for his classmates, his teachers, and his family. And when he found out he could make money simply doing what he loved, Leonardo was determined to break into show business.

It all began when Leo's stepbrother, Adam Starr, acted

Leo's character in *Parenthood* was based on the role Joaquin Phoenix played in the film version. By the time the series came out, Joaquin was too old for the role. Leo pursued the part of the interviewer in *Interview with the Vampire* after Joaquin's brother, River, died, leaving the role open. The producers decided Leo was too young for the part.

in a few commercials and made some serious cash. Leonardo then begged his parents to let him give it a shot. They made some appointments to try to get him an agent, but had trouble finding one who would sign him.

One agent even suggested he change his name to Lenny Williams. Imagine *Titanic*—the greatest love story ever told—starring Lenny Williams! But Leo refused to change his name. If he was going to be an actor, he was going to do it on his own terms.

Finally, with the help of a family friend, an agency signed Leonardo and he started to audition. He tried out for fifty commercials before he finally landed one for Matchbox cars when he was fourteen. After that he played an alcoholic teen on the soap opera *Santa Barbara*, had a bit part on *The New Lassie*, and worked on educational shorts like *How to Deal with a Parent Who Takes Drugs* and *Mickey's Safety Club*. He got his first big break when he won a role on the short-lived television series *Parenthood*.

Working on the show, Leo made friends with David Arquette (now famous for playing Dewey—the character who refuses to die in the *Scream* movies) and found himself on the pages of teen idol magazines like *Bop* and *16*. Unfortunately the show failed to find an audience and folded just a few months after it premiered. Leo told his agent he wanted another series.

That was when he found a job on one of the most

Leo at the *MTV Jock Jams.*

LEO'S GRANDMA, WHOM HE CALLS OMA, THINKS HER GRANDSON NEEDS TO PUT SOME MEAT ON HIS BONES.

successful sitcoms of the eighties, *Growing Pains*. The show had been at the height of its popularity when star Kirk Cameron was the nation's biggest poster boy. But now that Kirk was all grown up, the show's ratings had begun to drop, and the producers were looking for someone to bring back the young female audience. They chose Leo.

Clearly the producers had made a wise decision. Viewers responded to Leo immediately, and he was deemed a hot new Hollywood babe.

Leonardo still thought of himself as a scrawny little kid. He couldn't believe anyone would call him a hunk. When reporters visited the set of *Growing Pains* and asked him about his teen idol status, he rolled his eyes, playfully flexed his biceps, and said with a laugh, "Yeah, look at these muscles."

Leo enjoyed his time on the series, but there were rumors circulating that *Growing Pains* would be canceled at the end of the season, so Leo started auditioning for movies. He won roles in the small-budget features *Critters 3* and *Poison Ivy 2*. Then Leo tried out for the leading role in a little film called *This Boy's Life*. At the time he couldn't have known how quickly and profoundly his life was about to change. During a publicity tour for the movie Leo said, "Funny, but I thought that on my gravestone they were going to write, 'This was the guy from *Growing Pains*.'"

Boy, was he wrong.

Threads

Want to get this look (or help your boyfriend get it)?

Leo has mastered "fashionably hip" with his . . .

HOT HAIRCUT

Leo's messy trademark hair is called the **Shattered Look**. Just ask for it at your local salon. Leo's secret for keeping his 'do superslick is **Murray's Pomade**. You can find this cool little orange tin of styling goo at any drugstore.

UNSTRUCTURED DARK SUIT

Go to a vintage store! Guys might think this is crazy, but it's worth it! With a little luck and a bit of perseverance, you can find a great, inexpensive suit that will help you achieve this low-key lounge look. If there are no full suits available, try to find a single-breasted, oversized jacket—preferably navy blue or black. Or if you're really ready to heat things up, go for a pinstripe or a cool plaid. You might even be able to score a crisp, wing-collared shirt at the same place for a fraction of the cost of a new one.

WING-COLLARED, BUTTON-DOWN SHIRT

Another good choice for retro shirts is a company called **Plastic Idol**. They can be found at cool skate stores or specialty stores nationwide.

look is cool

The Basketball Diaries premiere, Westwood, CA.

This Boy's Rise to Fame

©1993 by Everett Collection

Even at the audition for *This Boy's Life*, Leonardo couldn't sit still. His friend Tobey Maguire was at the audition and said Leo was doing karate kicks in the hallway. "He wasn't serious at all," Maguire says. Tobey was sure Leo's unprofessional mischief was going to cost him the part. Not quite.

eo went in to read for the producers and the film's star, Oscar-winning actor Robert De Niro. "I stood up in front of De Niro really forcefully, and I pointed at his face and screamed one of the lines. Then I sat there and waited for some kind of reaction."

Well, the reaction was obviously positive . . . and long lasting. The moviemakers auditioned hundreds of hopefuls after Leo but kept coming back to his performance. Michael Caton-Jones, the director of the film, said, "I knew he was it, but when someone reads for you that early, you don't believe it." Luckily Caton-Jones decided to go with his heart and cast Leonardo in the part that would win him rave reviews.

"Young DiCaprio makes a very strong impression in his first leading role, [portraying] the many moods of adolescence with ease. Robert De Niro often seems forced in comparison," reads an on-line review. Leonardo, who knew of De Niro's highly acclaimed, award-winning work, must have been stunned by such praise, but he didn't let it go to his head. In fact, he underplayed his talent as an actor, saying all he saw was the negative stuff when he watched his own performance.

Leo in *What's Eating Gilbert Grape?*

Leonardo's Filmography

Celebrity (1998)
The Man in the Iron Mask (1998)
Titanic (1997)
Marvin's Room (1996)
William Shakespeare's Romeo and Juliet (1996)
Total Eclipse (1995)
Les cent et une nuits de Simon Cinéma (1995)
The Quick and the Dead (1995)
The Basketball Diaries (1995)
The Foot Shooting Party (1994)
What's Eating Gilbert Grape? (1993)
This Boy's Life (1993)
Poison Ivy 2 (1992)
Critters 3 (1991)
Growing Pains (1991–92) TV series
Parenthood (1990) TV series

But there wasn't much negative stuff to focus on in Leo's next film. His role as a mentally challenged boy named Arnie in 1993's *What's Eating Gilbert Grape?* earned him an Oscar nomination, a Golden Globe nomination, and numerous awards from critics' associations.

Suddenly the young actor was thrown into the spotlight, and he wasn't exactly comfortable with all the attention. Even though he used to improvise in front of tons of people when he was little, Leo had a terrible fear of speaking as himself in front of audiences. Leonardo said he was glad Tommy Lee Jones won the Academy Award the year he was nominated because he was so petrified he might have to get up onstage and speak. "No one was happier for [Tommy Lee] than me," Leo said.

But now Leonardo was a star, and there was no going back. His next few films, *The Basketball Diaries*, *The Quick and the Dead*, and *Total Eclipse*, might not have attracted large audiences, but Leo himself was developing a strong following.

Girls crowded the New York set of *The Basketball Diaries*, hoping to get a glimpse of Leonardo and his costar, Mark Wahlberg—then still known as Marky Mark the rap artist. This came as a shock to Leo. "I'd expect that for Marky, but for me it was bizarre," Leo said.

Meanwhile Mark and Leo "just clicked" and teamed up to make life on the set more interesting. They both loved to dance and mess around and even got caught throwing candy off a building in Hoboken, New Jersey, where some of the scenes were shot. But Leo was also learning to take his acting more seriously and spent a lot of time in New York's Greenwich Village, studying the local culture to make his performance more authentic. And he got to meet Jim Carroll—the real-life

Leo in *The Basketball Diaries*.

"THERE IS ONLY ONE REASON TO SEE THE GLOOMY, TRAGIC, BUT STRANGELY UNINVOLVING *THE BASKETBALL DIARIES*. THAT IS THE PERFORMANCE OF YOUNG LEONARDO DICAPRIO."

—Mal Vincent, movie critic, 1995

writer whom he played in the film. Leo grew to admire Jim and enjoyed going to poetry

they were interesting characters," Leo says. "If a movie's good, enough people will wind

"IF YOU'RE NOT PERFECT IN EVERY FILM, THEN PEOPLE SAY, 'SEE, HE WAS JUST LUCKY IN ONE ROLE.'"

—Leonardo DiCaprio

readings and book signings with him. In fact, Jim helped Leo choose the film *Total Eclipse* over a movie about legendary actor James Dean. *Total Eclipse* is the story of French poet Arthur Rimbaud, one of Carroll's favorite poets. But while Rimbaud is an idol in France, he's basically unknown in the United States, and *Total Eclipse* bombed with American audiences.

Still, Leo is proud of his work in both *Total Eclipse* and *The Basketball Diaries*. "If I had the choice again, I would still take those roles just because

up seeing it eventually— through whatever means. I don't really think about box office stuff that much."

Between *The Basketball Diaries* and *Total Eclipse* came Leonardo's first big-budget

James Madio, Mark Wahlberg, Patrick McGaw, and Leo in *The Basketball Diaries* (top). Leo with Ellen Barkin and Robert De Niro in *This Boy's Life* (above).

Leo with Mark Wahlberg at the premiere of *The Basketball Diaries*.

"DEALING WITH THEM IS LIKE BEING A WRANGLER."

—Liz Heller on Mark Wahlberg and Leonardo on the set of *The Basketball Diaries*

feature, *The Quick and the Dead*. At first Leo didn't want the part, but Sharon Stone, the film's star, wouldn't take no for an answer. Leo, who has often said that he takes his family and friends' advice on his career quite seriously, finally listened to their suggestions and took the role of "The Kid." The film didn't make much money, but it gave Leo the chance to work with Academy Award–winning actor Gene Hackman and future Golden Globe winner Stone. Leonardo also loved playing a cowboy.

These were all considered small films, but Leo worked on some even smaller projects during his first few years in movies. He starred in a twenty-minute-long film called *The Foot Shooting Party*. In it he played a 1970s hippie who shoots himself in the foot to avoid being drafted for the Vietnam War. He also made an appearance alongside Stephen Dorff, Harrison Ford, Robert De Niro, and Daryl Hannah in a French film called *Les cent et une nuits de Simon Cinéma* (*The One Hundred and One Nights of Simon Cinema*).

Leonardo in *The Quick and the Dead*.

Leonardo had made his mark in Hollywood as an actor who wasn't afraid to try challenging roles. In his next movie after *Total Eclipse*, Leo was to portray the most well-known romantic lead of all time—a role that had already been played by some of the most talented actors in the world.

And as always, Leo was up for the challenge.

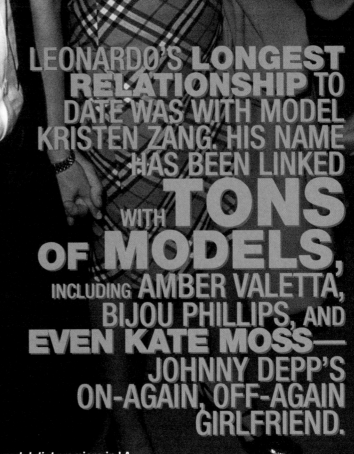

LEONARDO'S **LONGEST RELATIONSHIP** TO DATE WAS WITH MODEL KRISTEN ZANG. HIS NAME HAS BEEN LINKED WITH **TONS OF MODELS,** INCLUDING AMBER VALETTA, BIJOU PHILLIPS, AND **EVEN KATE MOSS—** JOHNNY DEPP'S ON-AGAIN, OFF-AGAIN GIRLFRIEND.

Leo and Kristen Zang at the *Romeo and Juliet* premiere in LA.

"I WOULDN'T HAVE DONE *ROMEO AND JULIET* IF IT HAD BEEN A PERIOD PIECE. MY FIRST THOUGHT WAS, 'WHY DO THIS AGAI

All Abou

Leo in *William Shakespeare's Romeo and Juliet.*

"

Director Baz Luhrmann gave Leo plenty of reasons to do the classic play again. He invited Leonardo to his homeland of Australia to work

Honor

through a few scenes, telling him if he didn't like it, he was welcome to pass. Leonardo took the trip and the chance and decided that Luhrmann's vision was fresh and hip enough to put a whole new spin on *Romeo and Juliet*. He then signed on to play one of the most famous and tragic romantic leads in literary history.

Finding the right leading lady wasn't easy, but when Claire Danes auditioned, she knocked both Baz and Leo off their feet. "She's really mature for her age," DiCaprio said around the time the film was released. (He was twenty-one and she was seventeen.) A lot of girls tried out for the role, but Leo said that their auditions weren't "nearly as truthful as Claire's performance."

And despite the fact that they had to battle major problems in Mexico, where the movie was filmed, Leo and Claire had a good time together on the set. They managed to get some thumb wrestling and club hopping in between the

"THEY JUST LIKE ME BECAUSE I GOT TO KISS LEO IN *ROMEO AND JULIET*."

—Claire Danes on her female fans

Leo with Claire Danes at the *Romeo and Juliet* premiere in Hollywood.

stomach viruses and killer bees that attacked the cast and crew.

DiCaprio was constantly hyper and fidgety on the set, chatting it up with makeup artists and wardrobe people, hosting parties in his hotel room, and flying his friends in from Los Angeles to hang out. But in front of the camera he was a total professional, delivering the tough Shakespearean lines as if he'd spoken that way from birth. His one complaint was that with all the swimming and rain scenes, he was getting sick of being wet. "I've been in the water so much, it's like an aquatic version of *Romeo and Juliet*," he said. After *Titanic*, Leo must look back on that comment and laugh.

William Shakespeare's Romeo and Juliet was a hit among teenage audiences with its hip, edgy, MTV-style take on the classic play. The movie finally made Shakespeare understandable to kids who had moaned and groaned over the play for

Leo in *Marvin's Room*.

"HE'S PROBABLY THE WORLD'S MOST BEAUTIFUL LOOKING MAN, BUT TO ME HE'S JUST SMELLY, FARTY LEO."

—Kate Winslet

Leo in *Titanic*.

Kate Winslet and Leo at the Golden Globe Awards.

"HE CAN'T TAKE COMPLIMENTS, ABSOLUTELY HATES THEM. HE GOES, **'SHUT UP'** AND GETS ME IN A HEADLOCK AND WRESTLES ME TO THE GROUND." —Kate Winslet

funny. He's like a light. He walks in and it's like magic," Keaton said.

Oddly, a couple of years later, *Titanic* director James Cameron would almost echo her words: "I met him and basically just loved him. He can quickly charm a group of people without doing anything obvious. . . . The second I met him I was convinced. It was like a shaft of light came down from the heavens."

James Cameron might have been certain that Leonardo was perfect to play Jack Dawson, choosing him over both Chris O'Donnell and Matthew McConaughy for the part, but Leo himself wasn't so sure. It was Kate Winslet, Leo's costar in *Titanic*, who persuaded him to take the role. "I was thinking, 'I'm going to persuade him to do this, because I'm not going to do it without him, and that's all there is to it. I will have him," Kate said.

Millions of fans are thankful to Kate for convincing Leonardo to be in *Titanic*. But there might have been times when Leo second-guessed his decision. The seven-month-long shoot was difficult, and if Leo had his fill of getting wet in *Romeo and Juliet*, you can imagine that filming some of the scenes in *Titanic* could have put him over the top.

Leo says that Kate was a major source of support during

years. And of course, the film made Leonardo DiCaprio the ultimate romantic hero for girls around the globe.

Girls were still waiting with pounding hearts for *R&J* to be released on video when Leonardo hit the big screen again with *Marvin's Room*. The film was geared toward an adult audience, but many of his younger fans went to see it as well. In the movie Leonardo plays a troubled teen who has to come to grips with the importance of family. His per-

formance had a lot of people talking Oscar nomination, but Leonardo was passed over that year. The film was a critical success, however, and Leonardo enjoyed working with world-class actresses Meryl Streep and Diane Keaton.

"I was in love with him. He's great, he's beautiful . . . so talented, so gifted and

Leo can't seem to get away from water. His Romeo first saw Juliet through an aquarium. He spent half of *Titanic* soaked. His favorite book is Hemingway's *The Old Man and the Sea*, and his perfect astrological love match is Pisces—the fish.

the shoot. "She was my best friend for seven months," he said. "We'd unload the stresses of the shoot to each other, vent to each other, watch out for each other. Kate was just the perfect person to work with because she was very much one of the guys, and it would have been much harder without her. We were partners."

Life on the set wasn't all serious—the stars managed to have some fun, too. When Leo wasn't trying to avoid the water and Kate wasn't freaking out about hanging in a harness a hundred feet over the ground, the two kept each other entertained. They would sing cheesy songs to each other, cuddle under blankets while looking at the stars, and play video games.

It's a good thing Leo and Kate had each other to laugh with because at the time, all of Hollywood was saying that *Titanic* was destined to sink like its namesake. Rumors about the production flew around town, claiming that the shoot had dangerous working conditions, that James Cameron was impossible to work with, and that the filming was way off schedule. Plus at $200 million, the movie wasn't simply overbudget—it was the most expensive film ever made. The studios that financed the movie were praying they'd just break even.

But one of Leo's friends wasn't so sure that *Titanic* was going to bomb. "Little does Leo know what's going to happen when *Titanic* comes out. I mean, it's huge. And it's not going to be just twelve-year-old girls watching him. It's

going to be everyone," Tobey Maguire said before the movie premiered.

He knew what he was talking about. The movie has been successful beyond everyone's expectations. *Titanic* broke every existing box office record, grossing over a billion and a half dollars worldwide, and won an astounding eleven Academy Awards, including Best Picture. Although Leonardo was snubbed by the Oscars, he won a Golden Globe nomination, incredible reviews, and the hearts of women everywhere.

Movieline magazine rated Leo's performance as the best among young actors in the past ten years, saying he was "quite simply the best actor of his generation." And the movie turned Leonardo into a reluctant A-list superstar.

"I'm just adjusting to it all. It's cool. I mean, it's different than anything else I've ever experienced for sure," Leo says. But above and beyond the special effects, the star-studded premieres, and the piles of money the film continues to rake in, Leonardo always wanted to make sure that

Leo and Kate Winslet in *Titanic*.

people remembered what was truly important and special to him about the movie—the love story.

"The film projects the love story in such a fantastic way, and that's what I'm most proud of—the fact that it didn't all get overshadowed," Leo said at the film's Los Angeles premiere.

Yet everywhere Leo went, it seemed that he was the one overshadowing everyone else— at least with the fans. His car was mobbed at the foreign premiere in Tokyo, and he had to be rushed in a side entrance by bodyguards. When asked what he thought about his millions of screaming fans, he said, "If it comes or if it goes, that's fine with me. I just want to keep

"HE HAS AN INNATE ABILITY TO GET **UNDER THE SKIN** OF A CHARACTER THAT I BELIEVE EVEN HE HIMSELF DOESN'T QUITE UNDER- STAND." —David Rubin, *R&J* casting director

Leo in *The Man in the Iron Mask*.

John Malkovich and Leo in *The Man in the Iron Mask*.

growing as an actor and doing good work. That's my main objective."

Leo's next role really gave him a chance to grow. In fact, he doubled himself. Leonardo played the cocky, evil king Louis XIV of France and his gentle, timid twin brother, Philippe, in *The Man in the Iron Mask*.

Filmed on location in France, the movie is full of sword fights, dark dungeons, and lavish palace scenery. Leonardo, who loves extreme sports like bungee jumping, skydiving, and racing all-terrain vehicles, enjoyed learning to use a sword and dueling with his costar, John Malkovich. Once again he got the chance to romance a beautiful woman on-screen.

This time it was French actress Judith Godreche.

> Leonardo rubbed elbows with royalty when he met Prince Charles at *Titanic*'s London premiere. He'd already played royalty, having wrapped his role as King Louis XIV in *The Man in the Iron Mask* a couple of months earlier.

Despite all the perks, including finally being on dry ground again, there was one thing about the shoot that bothered Leo—the mask. "It definitely gets claustrophobic. Within ten minutes of being in there I could almost bash my head against the wall in frustration," Leo said.

But even with the uncomfortable costumes, Leo was psyched to have the chance to work with such great actors, calling it a dream cast. And he also loved his role. "This is possibly the most fun character I've ever played in my life," Leo said.

On its opening weekend *The Man in the Iron Mask* tied *Titanic* as the number-one moneymaker for that weekend. *Titanic* was in its thirteenth week of release, and the first movie to challenge its number-one spot was another Leo film. Leonardo DiCaprio had turned into a movie producer's dream—a guaranteed moneymaker.

Still, Leo remained as unaffected as always. He took his mom to the star-studded

"I DON'T THINK THERE ARE ANY ANGELS IN THIS GROUP."

—John Malkovich on the cast of *The Man in the Iron Mask*

premiere of *The Man in the Iron Mask* in New York City. One lucky fan who made her way to the front of the crowd reached out and touched his hand. "He just turned to me and said, 'Hi. How are you doing?' and he held my hand for a second. Then he actually apologized because he couldn't stay. He said he had to get his mother inside. I couldn't believe how polite and calm he was with all those people screaming his name."

Leonardo the superstar was still Leonardo the gentleman.

Out of the Spotlight

As *Titanic* premiered to sold-out audiences, Leonardo was removing himself from the hype and talking about taking a break.

"You work for so long and you start to forget all the other interests you've had," Leo says. "And now's the time to sort of put them into action and forget about movies for a little bit."

All the craziness had finally gotten to the guy who values his quality time with his family and close friends. Still, Leo's name has been associated with many upcoming projects. In the fall of 1998 he appears in the next Woody Allen movie, *Celebrity*, which reunites him with Kate Winslet and also features Kim Basinger, Winona Ryder, Mira Sorvino, and Kenneth Branagh.

He's also been approached to star in a few other films. Both his name and Brad Pitt's have been connected to *Slay the Dreamer*, a story about a schizophrenic law student. There has also been talk of Leo playing Theodore Hall, a teenage genius who helped create the atom bomb, in *Bombshell*. Although nothing was definite at this writing, one thing is for sure: No matter what project Leonardo takes on next, he's going to give it his all.

"I want to try everything, as long as it's real," Leo says.

And judging by his popularity, the world is ready for everything Leonardo DiCaprio has to offer.

The Lowdown on Leo

Full name: Leonardo Wilhelm DiCaprio **Birth date:** November 11, 1974 **Birthplace:** Los Angeles, California **Astrological sign:** Scorpio **Height/weight:** 6 feet tall and about 150 pounds **Shoe size:** 11 **Nicknames:** Noodle, Leo (duh) **Favorite colors:** Black, purple, and dark green **Favorite foods:** Pasta, caramel corn, chocolate, and lemonade **Favorite bands:** Pink Floyd, The Beatles, Led Zeppelin (Get out your parents' record collection!) **Favorite pastimes:** Traveling, dancing, and playing pool, video games, and basketball **Favorite extreme sports:** Skydiving, bungee jumping, and in-line skating **Foreign language:** He's fluent in German **Favorite cities:** New York and San Francisco **Favorite pro sports team:** The Los Angeles Lakers **Favorite designers:** Prada, Fred Segal, and Mossimo **First car:** Jeep Grand Cherokee (he's had a few others since then) **Pets:** He has a lizard named Blizzard that almost died when it was run over on the set of *Titanic*. Luckily Leo was able to nurse Blizzard back to health. When he was little, he had a dog named Rocky. **Famous friends:** Alicia Silverstone, Kate Winslet, Claire Danes, Liv Tyler, Mark Wahlberg, Demi Moore, Sara Gilbert, Tobey Maguire, and magician David Blaine **Weakest body part:** His knees. He's going in for surgery in 1998. **Leo's collectibles:** Baseball cards as a kid. Sports cars as an adult **High school activities:** Drama club (no . . . really?), citizenship club, voted class clown **What he looks for in a friend:** People who are "real" **What he looks for in a girlfriend:** Someone intelligent and sweet who is "extremely understanding" **Favorite actors:** Robert De Niro, Al Pacino, Jack Nicholson, John Malkovich, and Meg Ryan **Favorite icon:** James Dean **Big move:** He moved out of his mom's house in November 1997 and got his own pad. **Cool Leo website:** www.leonardodicaprio.com **On-set victory:** Convinced Baz Luhrmann not to make the actors in-line skate through *William Shakespeare's Romeo and Juliet* **On-set tragedy:** He was kicked off the set of *Romper Room* at age five for being too rowdy **First kiss:** Hated it! Too much saliva **Biggest gift ever given:** He built a house for his mom in West Virginia **Why he wants to take a break:** Thirteen films in seven years? You'd want some time off, too! **Tattoo:** He doesn't have a permanent one, but he's been known to slap on a temporary. **Event that "made a man" of him:** Filming *Titanic* **Dramatic training:** Experience only. He's never taken an acting class. **Body double:** Those weren't Leo's hands drawing Kate's portrait in *Titanic*. They were director James Cameron's **Does he believe in love at first sight?** You bet!